For Toby, Isla, and Jesse — A. D.

For my father — V. S.

• First U.S. edition 2013 • Library of Congress Catalog Card Number pending • ISBN 978-0-7636-6608-8 Printed in Heshan, Guangdong, China • This book was typeset in Franklin Gothic. • The illustrations were done in pencil and digitally colored. • Candlewick Press, 99 Dover Street, Somerville, Massachusetts 02144 • visit us at www.candlewick.com •

13 14 15 16 17 18 LEO 10 9 8 7 6 5 4 3 2 1

CANDLEWICK PRESS

CHEESE BELONGS TO YOU!

Alexis Deacon illustrated by **Viviane Schwarz**

THIS IS RAT LAW:

Cheese belongs to **you.**

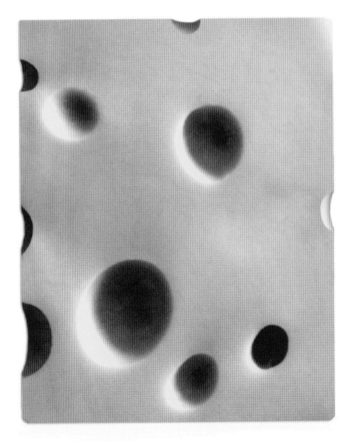

Unless a **big** rat wants it.
Then cheese belongs to him.

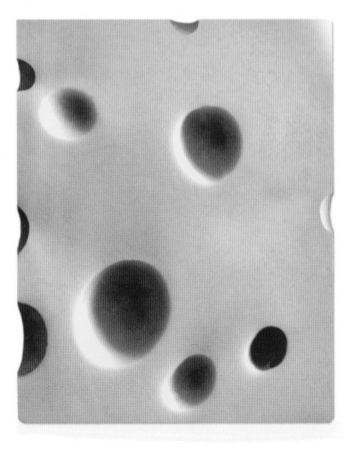

Unless a **bigger** rat wants it.
Then cheese belongs to her.

Unless a quicker rat wants it . . .

or a **stronger** rat wants it . . .

or a **SCARY** rat . . .

or a **hairy** rat . . .

or a dirty rat . . .

or a dirty, hairy rat . . .

or a dirty, hairy, scary rat . . .

or a big, quick, strong, scary, hairy, dirty rat.

If a big, quick, strong, scary, hairy, dirty rat wants it, then **cheese** belongs to her.

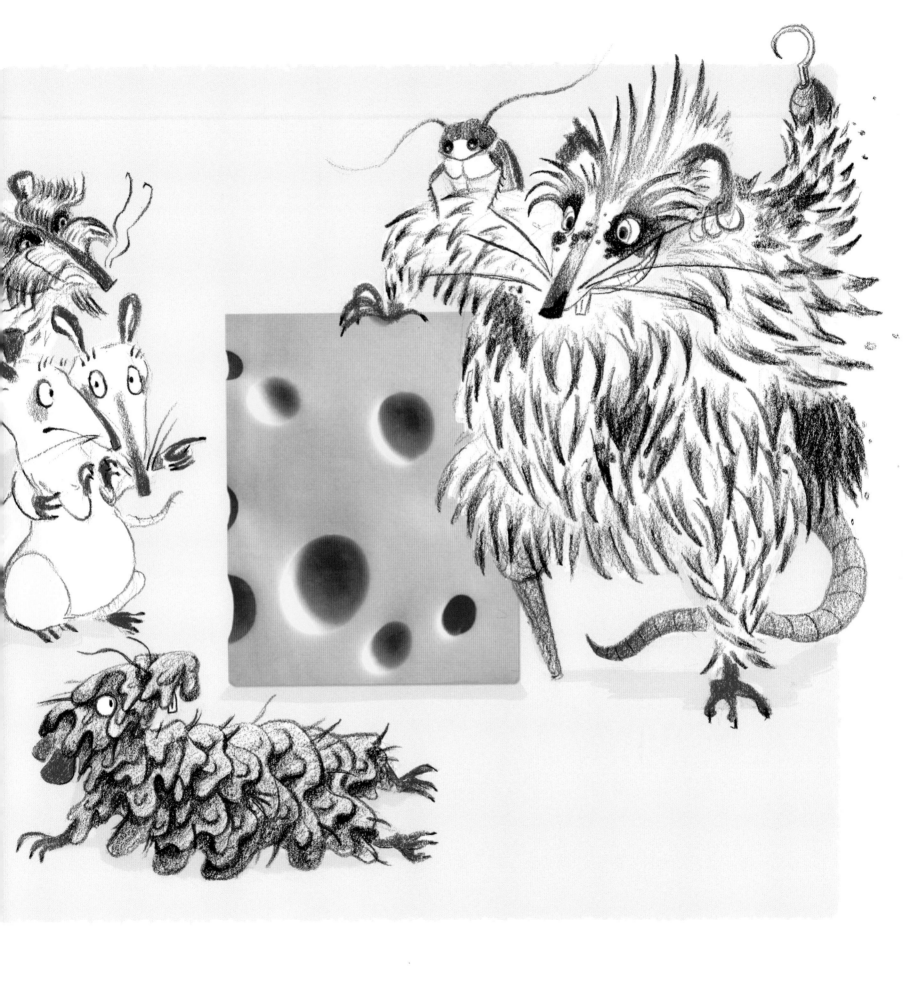

Unless a gang of rats wants it.

Unless a gang of big, quick, strong, scary, hairy, dirty rats wants it.

Unless the biggest gang of the biggest, quickest, strongest, scariest, hairiest, dirtiest rats wants it.

Unless the boss of the biggest, quickest, strongest, scariest, hairiest, dirtiest rats wants it.

If the boss of the biggest, quickest, strongest, scariest, hairiest, dirtiest rats wants it, then cheese belongs to him.

Unless . . .

someone **else** wants to be boss.

Now cheese belongs to you again . . .

if you still want it. **THAT IS RAT LAW.**

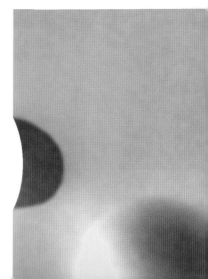

Would anybody else like some, too?